This book belongs to

_____

Spider Spins a Story

FOURTEEN LEGENDS *from* NATIVE AMERICA

Edited by JILL MAX

Illustrations by

ROBERT ANNESLEY • BENJAMIN HARJO • MICHAEL LACAPA • S.D. NELSON
REDWING T. NEZ • BAJE WHITETHORNE

rising moon

Books for Young Readers from Northland Publishing

To our mothers,

Mary Ellen and Sara.

Like the spider,

"You make your house and all things come to it."

The text type was set in Weiss
The display type was set in Quetzalcoatl
Composed in the United States of America
Designed by Mary C. Wages
Art Directed by Rudy J. Ramos
Edited by Tom Carpenter and Erin Murphy
Production Supervised by Lisa Brownfield

Manufactured in China by Regent Publishing Services Ltd.

FIRST IMPRESSION
ISBN 0-87358-611-5

Library of Congress Catalog Card Number pending

0585/7.5M/7-97

Contents

⌄▵▵▵⌄▵⌄▵⌄

Preface

by Jill Max

Sadly, many Native Americans have been denied knowledge of their distinct tribal histories and cultures. Tribes have been separated, relocated, and some annihilated. Indians fortunate enough to have stayed with their tribes have formed images of their people functioning within different environments, in different parts of North America, and in radically different tribal structures from those in which the tribes existed when these legends were first told.

It is only recently that many people of American Indian ancestry have had the opportunity and freedom to reconnect with their roots. To this end, we have added details about clothing, dwellings, landscape, and hunting-and-gathering practices to the legends in this book, so the reader may experience the stories more fully. These additions were made only after consulting the storytellers and tribal members to verify all details, and most importantly, to be sure the additions do not alter the meaning and spirit inherent in the legends. All bands, clans, families, and tribes do not tell the legends in exactly the same way; likewise, different storytellers tell varying versions of the same legend. Because a particular legend is told one way in this book is not meant, in any way, to discredit another version or storyteller. The significance of each version is important and should be valued and preserved as such.

In gratitude for being allowed to share these stories and out of respect and support for the struggle of all American Indians to hold onto their cultures, we have chosen to donate one-third of our earnings from *Spider Spins a Story* to the American Indian Theater Company, a multi-tribal organization whose goal is to preserve and share Native American culture and history.

Spider Spins a Story is similar to the legends it brings together. It doesn't belong to any individual; it is part of every person who helped us gather information, told us a story, provided guidance and encouragement, made a phone call, or mailed a letter. You hold this volume in your hands because American Indian culture has a rich history of storytellers and stories. So many people, slightly touched by the spider, helped us weave those silken story threads together.

A few of the storytellers we worked with wish to remain anonymous. They felt putting a "name" on a story denoted ownership; each story belongs to the whole tribe, not only to the storyteller or the person who writes it down. We thank them. The gestures, phrasing, intonation, sounds, and expressions of each storyteller bring these legends to life. Storytelling is, after all, a performing art, and to be truly appreciated, a story must be told to an audience. We thank each of the storytellers we worked with for allowing us to watch and listen to them practice their art, naming among them Shan Goshorn, Will Hill, Ed Ramon, Jake Chanate, Archie Mason, Cricket Rhodes, Sam Hart, and Dale Childs, who mesmerized us while they unfolded their stories; and Sarah Natani, who was our catalyst.

Likewise, we could not let this book go without sending thanks to Sean StandingBear, Dr. Chris Cavender, Jim Rementer, Alph Secakuku, Michael Lacapa, Rita Edaakie, Imogene Mosquedo, Louis Johnson, and Dr. Garrick Bailey for their patience and expertise.

We thank also Monetta and Robert Trepp and all those connected with the American Indian Theater Company; Roberta at the Pawnee Tribal Office; Glenda Galvan at the Chickasaw/Choctaw Cultural Center; Linda Kakuska, Bernadette Huber, Brad Lerschen, Nancy Cawee, and Merle Haas on the Wind River Reservation; Radley Davis, Sheila Montgomery, and Marian L. Bowie of the Bear River Band; and Darlene Buckley and Cheryl Seidner, for their smiling voices on the other end of the telephone line.

To the research librarians on the third floor at the Central Library in Tulsa; to Sarah, hidden away in the Gilcrease Museum Archives; and to Dolores Sumner at Northeastern State University; thanks for taking time to look up all the obscure tidbits we needed "right now!" Ah-ho to Evans Ray, Perry, and the rest of the Tuesday Night Kiowa Language Class for bringing us into your circle, and sharing your language and customs, *tsoy*, and songs.

Thanks to Erin Murphy and Tom Carpenter, our editors at Northland. Erin, your strong belief in the project made this book a reality.

And last, but not least, thanks to our families for supporting and indulging our obsession.

The Great Flood

A KIOWA LEGEND

illustrated by Benjamin Harjo

"The Great Flood" is the first section of the Kiowa's Sacred Story Cycle. It has been previously published and appears here with permission from Evans Ray Satepauhoodle, an elder of the Southern Kiowa tribe.

In the Kiowa language, Grandmother Spider is called Kawna-tawh-mah. According to Kiowa Voices, Vol. II: Myths, Legends, and Folktales, by Maurice Boyd, corn, a staple of the Native American diet, first grew in the garden of Grandmother Spider. Grandfather Snake is called Con-te'y sahn-nay; he is also referred to as "Stony Road" because he leaves a rough, wiggly trail on the ground.

Long ago, the spirit powers became angry. In their rage, they unleashed a mighty storm that ravaged the earth. It rained for ten days. The water covered the land and every living thing was washed away.

Only two beings were able to survive the great flood, Grandmother Spider and Grandfather Snake. Grandmother Spider lived because she was light and could float with her many legs on top of the water. Grandfather Snake survived because he could slither through the water.

When the rains ceased and the waters soaked into the earth, Grandmother Spider and Grandfather Snake became husband and wife.

After a time, Grandmother Spider planted a garden. All the grasses, fruits, vegetables, flowers, and trees living on the earth today first grew in the garden of Grandmother Spider.

How the Tewas Found Their True Home

A TEWA LEGEND

illustrated by Michael Lacapa

Known as the "Moccasin People," the Tewas are a Pueblo tribe who make their home in the Upper Rio Grande Valley between Santa Fe and Taos, New Mexico. They depend on the river for fishing, and for irrigation water for their crops. Tewas villages have four dance plazas (one for each of the four directions) built around the sacred center of the village. The sacred center symbolizes the spot where the Tewas emerged from the Middle Place.

"How the Tewas Found their True Home" is a shortened version of the Tewa creation story. Traditionally, a much longer version is told in winter, the proper storytelling time. This legend illustrates Grandmother Spider in her customary role as "the Earth Goddess, an underground being of extraordinary powers who's friendly to man" (from Dictionary of Mythology, Folklore, and Symbols, *by Gertrude Jobes).*

ong, long ago, the Tewas spent their days wandering the universe, for they had no home. Their warrior leader, Long Sash (the constellation Orion), heard of a land far away where they could settle. He led his people on a dangerous journey across the sky. At the end of the Endless Trail (the beltway of stars called the Milky Way), they came to a place of darkness. Here, Long Sash left the Tewas, for his place was in the Sky World.

The Tewas wandered about in this world of darkness. As time passed, they began to wonder if there was a different world somewhere—a place where life was more than just crawling around like bugs in the blackness.

While they were wondering, Mole came by, digging through the dark with sharp claws. "You travel all over," the Tewas said to Mole. "Tell us, in your travels, have you found a different world from this?"

"It is true no other travels as much as I," answered Mole. "Sometimes I dig down and sometimes I dig up. When I dig up, I come to a place that feels different. Since I'm blind, I cannot see if that is truly a different world. I could lead you to that place so you could look around."

"How will we know when we reach the new place?" they asked.

"When I feel the air change, I will tell you," said Mole.

The Tewas followed Mole as he dug his way up through the underground. But they did not need Mole to tell them when they reached the different world. The light from the Blue Sky World shined so brightly, it hurt the Peoples' eyes. They cried and covered their eyes with their hands. Some of them were so frightened by the brightness that they tried to climb back into the underground. But Mole had left, pushing the earth behind him as he crawled so that the hole to the underground was completely gone.

"What will we do now?" cried the Tewas. "At least when we were in the darkness we could see where we were."

"Be patient, my children, and I will help you," said a small voice.

"Who are you?" asked the terrified Tewas.

"I am Spider Woman, the Grandmother of the Earth," replied the voice. "Slowly take your hands away from your eyes, but only for a moment."

The people did as Grandmother Spider told them. Three times they took their hands away from their eyes. Each time they could see a little better. The fourth time, when they took their hands away, the light didn't hurt at all.

"Now that you can see, look there." Grandmother Spider pointed to a field of tall, green stalks. "That is k'un, corn. It is food for my people. To survive in the Blue Sky World, you must learn to plant k'un and care for it. You must work hard for the k'un. If you do, you will never know hunger."

"Where should we plant the k'un?" asked the Tewas. "Where should we make our home?"

Grandmother Spider seemed not to hear their questions. She climbed back into her web and began spinning. After awhile, though, she called down to the oldest among them. "Look to the east," she said. "See those red mountains? Those are the Red Eastern Mountains. The mountains are stained red from the blood of people who died fighting there. Stay away from those mountains or you, too, will be killed."

Most of the Tewas vowed to stay away from the Red Eastern Mountains, but a few thought the bright red ridges rising out of the flat, brown earth were very beautiful.

Awhile later, little Grandmother Spider stopped spinning again. "Look to the north," she said. "That mountain is called Mountain Standing. Your children will always be cold there, and k'un planted that far north will never grow tall."

Some of the Tewas, having never seen snow or felt the icy fingers of winter, thought the blanket of white covering Mountain Standing was very inviting.

"What about that mountain to the west, Grandmother Spider?" asked the old ones. "Should we travel west to that black mountain?"

Grandmother Spider once more stopped spinning so she could talk to the Tewas. "Black Mountain West is not a good place for your people. As the day passes, the sun moves across the sky toward Black Mountain. That is the place where the sun lays down to die. K'un planted there will wilt before it can ripen."

"We should never have come to this Blue Sky World!" cried some of the Tewas. "Life was not good for us underground, but at least we were not afraid."

All through the first night the Tewas spent in the Blue Sky World, they huddled together discussing Grandmother Spider's words and wondering where they should make their home.

The next morning, when the sun's rays began to burn the Red Eastern Mountains, Grandmother Spider stopped spinning one last time. In a voice that had become very soft and scratchy from so much talking, she said, "Look to the south. Far in the distance is Turtle Mountain. It is a golden place. When you have reached it, you will have reached your true home."

The People peered into the distance, trying to see as far as they could. "We can see something golden," they said, "but it doesn't really look like anything. How will we know when we have reached our new home?"

"When you find signs of your two friends again," said Grandmother Spider. "When you find signs of Mole, who led you into the Blue Sky World, and of me, Grandmother Spider, then you will know you have found your true home."

The Tewas thanked Grandmother Spider and set off. They had not traveled far when they began to quarrel. Those Tewas who had not listened well to Grandmother Spider left the group to go east; some headed north, and others headed west.

And, just as Grandmother Spider had warned, those who journeyed to the Red

Mountains East were killed by rampaging Comanches. If you look east in the summer sky, you will see a war bonnet left by one of the warriors.

And true to Grandmother Spider's words, those Tewas who journeyed north to Mountain Standing were frozen when White Bear came down from his home on the mountain and breathed his icy breath over them. Sometimes, on cold winter nights, you can see White Bear guarding his mountain.

Those Tewas who followed the sun as it crossed the sky met the angry War Twins when they reached Black Mountain. The War Twins waved their weapons at the people and shouted, "Go back, you foolish people! Didn't you listen to Grandmother's words? This is where the sun lies down to die. You cannot make your home here."

Late at night in the springtime, if you look in the sky you can see the Twins above Black Mountain.

The Tewas who ran from the Twins returned to find Grandmother Spider, but she was not there. That night, they learned where she had gone. There, in the center of her star web in the sky, sat Grandmother Spider, shaking her head because her people were so foolish, and crying star tears. The people cried too, and ran up the Endless Trail and into the sky to be with Grandmother Spider. On dark summer nights you can see those people, and if you look beyond the Endless Trail, you can see the spider's web.

Those Tewas who had listened well to Grandmother Spider traveled through many different lands—lands of dancing trees, rainbow-colored cliffs, and sandy, dusty deserts. The wind blew them and the sun baked them. Hot and tired and far from anything they knew, the People kept their footsteps always pointing south toward the golden gleam in the distance that Grandmother Spider had called Turtle Mountain.

The closer the People came to the golden mountains, the more worried they became. "So far we haven't seen signs of Grandmother Spider or Mole. Harm could come to us if these are the wrong mountains," they said.

One day the Tewas stopped to rest under a clump of cottonwood trees growing beside a river. After drinking some of the cool water and lying beneath the trees for a time, the people felt stronger and made ready to continue their journey.

"Look!" they said, noticing some small tracks. "Those are like Mole's claw marks!"

The People followed the tracks. Soon, they came upon a strange creature crawling through the sand.

"See the little creature's back!" the Tewas cried. "It is hard and round and has a design carved into it. The design looks like Grandmother Spider's web!"

"These are the signs Grandmother Spider told us to watch for," said the old ones.

"Look!" The People pointed up to the mountain. "The mountain has the same shape as the little creature. The creature must be a turtle and that must be Turtle Mountain, the golden mountain Grandmother Spider sent us to find. At last we have found our true home."

The Tewas settled there, in the shadow of Turtle Mountain beside the Rio Grande. And still, to this day, that is the place the Tewas call home.

Swift Runner and Trickster Tarantula

A ZUNI LEGEND

∧·∧·∧·∧·∧·∧·∧·∧

illustrated by Baje Whitethorne

The Zunis are a farming people who have been largely concentrated in one large village in westernmost New Mexico since the 1700s. Traditional Zuni homes are flat-roofed, apartment-like, adobe structures with no doors and rooftop openings accessible only by ladder, probably designed to protect them from enemies. While Zuni customs and lifestyle are similar to those of other Pueblo tribes, their language is very different. The Zunis are well known for their silver-and-turquoise jewelry.

Zunis believe anyone who ventures near Spider Woman's home comes under her powers. If untrained, that person may never be seen in the mortal world again. However, if visitors show her proper respect, as in this story, Spider Woman might use her magical powers or call upon her grandsons to assist them.

This Zuni legend has two spider figures: Tarantula, the trickster, and Spider Woman, the grandmother of the two war gods. The twin gods and Spider Woman are the only creatures whose medicine is powerful enough to trick Tarantula.

Many, many grandfathers ago, there was only one tarantula. He was a big, hairy spider, as big as a man, who dressed in ragged, gray-blue clothing. Tarantula lived in a cave at the base of Thunder Mountain.

Every sunrise, Tarantula was awakened by the sound of hornbells. He knew the bells were part of the sacred regalia worn by a young Zuni man called Swift Runner. Swift Runner, son of a Zuni priest-chief, would someday take his father's place. Each morning before prayers, Swift Runner dressed himself in his sacred garments and raced as fast as he could around Thunder Mountain so that when the time came, he would be strong enough to dance the strenuous prayer dances of the chiefs.

Tarantula envied Swift Runner's white-fringed leggings and the feathers tied in his hair. He envied him his belt of hornbells and his magnificent sparkling necklaces and earrings. Tarantula spent much of the day wondering how he could trick away Swift Runner's resplendent regalia.

One morning, as the red streaks of dawn reached upward in the eastern sky above the distant mesas, Tarantula waited for Swift Runner to appear.

"Young friend," he called, as Swift Runner ran toward him. "Come here. I want to talk to you."

"I must hurry or I will not complete my run before prayers," said Swift Runner.

"I will not delay you long," said Tarantula.

Impatiently, Swift Runner stopped. "What do you want?" he asked.

"You have the most beautiful clothing I've ever seen," said Tarantula. "I wish you could see yourself the way I see you."

Though Swift Runner was in a hurry, curiosity got the better of him. "How can I?" he asked.

"Take off your clothing," said Tarantula, "and I will take off mine. Then I will put on your regalia so you can see how splendid you look."

Swift Runner was young and foolish. He didn't know what a trickster Tarantula was. He laid his hornbell belt, his earrings and necklaces, his braided, many-colored headband, and his finely crafted moccasins, along with the rest of his sacred clothing, on the ground.

As fast as Swift Runner set down his finery, Tarantula dressed himself in the beautiful garments.

"How do I look?" asked Tarantula, struggling to fit his eight knobby legs and round, hairy body into Swift Runner's clothes.

Swift Runner took a long look at Tarantula. "I don't think the regalia looks quite the same on me," he said.

"If I move away, you will see it better," said Tarantula. He backed toward the entrance to his cave. "How do I look now?"

"Better," said Swift Runner. "But it's still hard to imagine that the regalia looks the same on me."

"Let me move back a little farther," said Tarantula. "Now look at me."

"Splendid!" said Swift Runner.

"Aha!" Tarantula turned quickly and disappeared into his cave.

"Come out!" cried Swift Runner. "I must be on my way and I need my regalia."

Swift Runner could hear Tarantula laughing from deep within the cave. No matter how much Swift Runner coaxed and cajoled, Tarantula would not come out.

When Swift Runner realized he'd been outsmarted, he did the only thing he could. He put on Tarantula's dingy brown leggings, breechcloth, and cape and returned home.

His father, the priest-chief, was waiting for him. "Where have you been, Swift Runner? And why are you dressed so shabbily?"

"Tarantula tricked me," said Swift Runner. "He took my sacred clothing and disappeared into his cave."

"We'll ask the warrior-chief," said his father. "He will know how to get your sacred clothing back from Tarantula."

The warrior-chief gathered the Zuni people together. "Bring your digging sticks to the cave at Thunder Mountain. We will dig Tarantula out."

From sundown to sunup to sundown, the people dug. Dirt piled in mounds around them. They dug all the way to the solid rock core of Thunder Mountain, but there was no sign of Tarantula.

When the people returned to the village, Swift Runner's father called on the elders for help.

"Let's seek the advice of the Great Kingfisher," said the elders. "We have seen the way he swoops down and snatches even the fastest fish out of the river. Kingfisher will know how to retrieve Swift Runner's clothing."

Flying like the wind, Swift Runner set out at once for the hill where Kingfisher lived.

"Tarantula is very cunning and keen-sighted," said Kingfisher. "It will not be easy to get your clothes back, but I will try my best."

Kingfisher flew to Thunder Mountain and hid opposite the cave. With only the tip of his bill showing between twin columns of rock, he watched for Tarantula.

Finally, Tarantula strutted out of the cave wearing Swift Runner's regalia. He looked all around to see if anyone was watching. His keen eyes spotted the tip of Kingfisher's bill.

"Aha! I see you hiding there," said Tarantula.

Kingfisher spread his wings and swooped down upon Tarantula, but Tarantula was too fast. Kingfisher had barely brushed the feathers on Tarantula's headdress when Tarantula jumped back into his hole, laughing with glee.

The sound of Tarantula's victory song followed Kingfisher as he flew back to the Zuni village.

"My best was not good enough," said Kingfisher. "There is nothing more I can do."

The elders sent for Great Eagle.

"Your eyes are seven times sharper than the eyes of our people," said the elders. "Will you help us get back Swift Runner's sacred clothing?"

Eagle sharpened his talons. "Tarantula is cunning and keen-sighted, as my brother, Kingfisher, said, but I will do my best."

From his high perch on a distant peak, Eagle kept first one eye and then the other on Tarantula's cave. He watched and waited.

He didn't have to wait long. The moment Tarantula poked his hairy head out of the opening, Eagle dove at him. But Tarantula saw Eagle coming. Before Eagle's talons could do more than pluck a feather from Tarantula's headdress, the speedy spider had ducked back into his cave.

"What a well-dressed, clever trickster I am!" sang Tarantula, dancing a victory dance.

Sadly, Eagle flew back to the Zuni village.

"You are our last hope, Falcon," said the elders. "You are the fastest of the feathered beings. You are quicker than Kingfisher and as mighty as Eagle. With your brown and gray feathers the color of rocks, Tarantula will not see you. Surely, you can get Swift Runner's sacred clothing back."

"I will try my best," said Falcon.

The next morning, when Tarantula poked his ugly face out of the cave, he saw nothing. Thinking he was safe, he stepped away from the opening.

Falcon flew down upon Tarantula and before Tarantula knew what had happened, Falcon snatched away the feathered headdress.

Shaking with fright, Tarantula crawled back into his cave. "Oh, my glorious feathers are gone!" he cried. "But luckily that nasty Falcon did not take my fine shirt, handsome leggings, and beautiful moccasins. They are worth far more than a fistful of feathers. I am still the best-dressed and cleverest trickster!"

Falcon carried the feathered headdress back to the Zuni village. "This is the best I could do," he said.

"Thank you," said Swift Runner. "These feathers are very precious to me."

"There's only one thing left to do," said the elders. "Swift Runner, you must journey to the top of Thunder Mountain and ask for help from the war gods, Ahaiyuta and Matsailema. Maybe they can get your sacred clothes back from Tarantula."

The Zuni villagers bundled together their most valuable possessions for Swift Runner to take as gifts for the gods.

It was late in the day when Swift Runner reached the flat-roofed house where the war gods lived with their grandmother, Spider Woman.

"A young man is here," Spider Woman said, calling the war gods from their games. "He has brought gifts."

The two tiny war gods, small as dwarfs, sat down across from Swift Runner. "No stranger comes to another's house for no reason," they said. "Why have you come?"

"I bring gifts from my people," said Swift Runner. "I also bring you a problem and hope for your help. Tarantula has stolen my sacred clothing. Great Kingfisher, Great Eagle, and Falcon have all tried to get it back and failed."

"It is good you came," said the war gods. "Only we can out-trick the trickster Tarantula."

Spider Woman gathered white sandstone rocks and ground them until they were as fine as flour. Then she added water to the flour and made a dough. Amazed, Swift Runner watched the two war gods mold the dough into two deer and two antelope.

"Tarantula loves to hunt," explained the war gods. "Take these animals and place them on a rock shelf across from Tarantula's cave."

Swift Runner did as he was told. Then he returned to the village. "Make yourselves ready," he said to the people.

The Zuni warriors sharpened their arrows and restrung their bows. Before dawn, the war party set out.

Swift Runner was the first to arrive at Thunder Mountain. To his surprise, the rock-and-flour animals had come to life. They were walking along the ledge, nibbling grass.

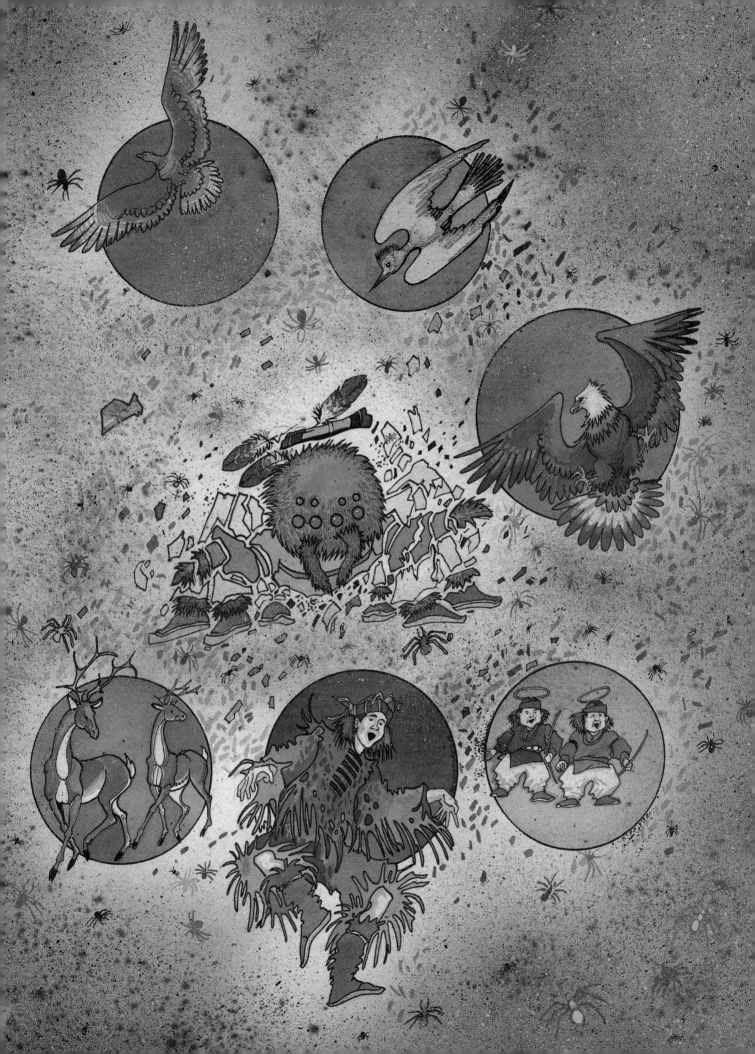

At sunrise, Tarantula came out of his cave. "Ah! Deer and antelope!" he said. "It is time for a hunt!"

He picked up his bow and arrow and was about to leave when he stopped himself. "Swift Runner will be looking for me. I must be careful."

Tarantula searched behind the twin columns where Kingfisher had hidden. He peered across at the tall peak where Eagle had perched. He strained to catch sight of Falcon's rock-colored feathers. He looked up and down the valley. "If my keen eyes see no one, there is no one!"

Tarantula pulled back on his bowstring and aimed. He felled the first deer with his first arrow. The second arrow struck the heart of the second deer. The third and fourth arrow downed the two antelope. "What a great hunter I am!" he boasted.

Tarantula lashed together the legs of the first deer and hoisted it onto his back. Just as he started to rise, he was knocked flat and almost crushed.

"Yiiii!" he cried. "What happened?"

Tarantula looked around. The deer was gone. Piled on his back and all around him was white sandstone.

Tarantula picked up the other deer. The instant he lifted it onto his back, the deer changed into white sandstone and knocked him flat.

"These deer have some sort of magic," he said. "I will try an antelope."

But like the deer, the first antelope turned to sandstone.

As Tarantula was tying the legs of the last antelope, he heard shouting. Zuni warriors were swarming into the canyon. Tarantula left the antelope and ran as fast as his knobby legs could carry him toward his cave.

The warriors blocked the entrance. Surrounding Tarantula, they tore off Swift Runner's braided headband and his beautiful moccasins. They yanked the earrings from Tarantula's ears until he screamed in pain.

"Please, don't hurt me!" cried Tarantula. "I will give Swift Runner back his clothing if you will just leave me alone."

"Tarantula is too cunning and clever, too big and powerful to be allowed to go free," said the elders. "The only way to rid the world of Tarantula and his trickery is to roast him!"

The people built an enormous fire, so large it lit up the sky like a sunset. When the fire was as hot as a fire can get, they threw the big, hairy, knobby-legged spider into the flames. He sizzled and hissed, he screamed and swelled. He swelled into a gigantic gray-blue ball.

Tarantula had one trick left. When he burst, he exploded into millions of pieces— each piece becoming a tiny version of trickster Tarantula himself.

How the Spider Got Its Web

A WIYAT LEGEND

illustrated by Robert Annesley

The Wiyats (also spelled Wiyots) are a small tribe whose traditional lands are located in the Humboldt Bay area (along the northern coast of California) in the heart of the redwood forest. The Wiyats used these tall, red-barked trees to make canoes and build their homes. Most of their food came from the ocean: salmon, whales, and shellfish. They also gathered nuts and berries and hunted small game. The Wiyats are known for their exceptional basket weaving.

In the spider stories of the tribes of the Northwest Coast, the spider maintains a true spider form. Using their spider traits—web, small size, climbing ability—spiders aid the people and other animals.

I n a time when the world was new, all the animals were well fed and content except Spider. Spider's belly growled with hunger, but he didn't know how to get food. He decided to ask Old Man Above for help.

Climbing a tall redwood that had poked a hole into sky country, Spider went to look for Old Man Above. Spider found him sitting on a tule-reed mat, twisting hair into string.

"I'm hungry," complained Spider. Old Man Above began winding the string into a ball.

"I don't have any way to catch food," continued Spider. "You gave Grizzly Bear sharp claws and powerful jaws. You gave Beaver long, strong teeth. You gave Red Fox quickness and cunning. But you made me small and weak. How am I to eat?"

Old Man Above peered down at the squeaky little creature. "Take this," he said, giving Spider the ball of string.

"A ball of string is neither teeth nor claws, quickness nor cunning," said Spider. "How will it feed me?"

"Just as Grizzly Bear learned to use his claws, Beaver learned to use his teeth, and Red Fox learned to use his quickness and cunning, you must learn to use your gift." Old Man Above rose to his feet. "Now go away and don't bother me again," he said, disappearing into the clouds.

Spider pulled his hair with his eight legs. "I came all this way and I'm no better off than I was before! What kind of gift is a ball of string?" Spider's stomach grumbled in answer. Angrily, he stuffed the string into his mouth.

When he had gobbled up the whole ball, Spider heaved a sigh. His belly was full and silent at last. He was ready to go home.

Spider searched all over sky country, but he couldn't find the place where the redwood poked through the clouds.

Suddenly, the sky began to shake.

"It's Old Man Above!" cried Spider. "What will he do if he finds me still here?"

Spider cleared a spot in the clouds and peered down at the ground far below. "If I hadn't eaten the ball of string," he said, "I could use it to get down."

The clouds trembled as Old Man Above drew closer.

Gulping in fear, Spider felt the string tickling the back of his throat. Frantically, he spit out a bit of the string and tied it to the edge of the sky. As the string unraveled, Spider clung to it with all of his eight legs. He lowered himself to the ground and scampered home.

From then until now, every Spider carries the gift of string from Old Man Above. Using it to make a web, Spider catches his food and is never hungry.

Osage Spider Story

AN OSAGE LEGEND

‹·∧·∧·∧·∧·∧·∧·›

told by Archie Mason, Jr., *illustrated by* Redwing T. Nez

The Osages are a Sioux tribe that originally lived in an area north and west of the Mississippi, in what is now southern Missouri and northern Kansas. They lived much like other Plains Indians, except their villages were permanent and they farmed. Today the Osage Nation is centered in Oklahoma. Osage legends are simple teaching stories. They are the tribe's history. The Osages have no alphabet and have always relied on the power of storytelling.

The spider is a respected symbol to the Osages. According to Francis La Flesche, author of The Osage Tribe, the spider is the life symbol for the Isolated Earth People, the earliest known Osages. The Osage spider is a giant wood spider about six inches in diameter. According to Osage myth, the spider's web is like a snare that traps all living things and holds them here on earth until they die.

The Osages have a complex social organization. Stories vary depending on the clans' interpretation. This version is told by the Sky Clan.

his is what happened back in the times when animals and insects could talk; or, I should say, back in the times when we, the *Wa-zha-zhe,* the Osage, knew how to listen.

The spiders, honeybees, yellow jackets, and mud daubers: these insects still speak—a language that is older than humans. The buffalo, elk, wolf, coyote—they still talk, too. It's we, the people, who have forgotten how to listen.

Back in those times, the Wa-zha-zhe walked this earth. We trapped and hunted with hardwood bows and arrows. From animal hides we made leggings and moccasins to protect our legs and feet. From the fur of these animals we made wraps to cover ourselves when the cold winds blew. From tall prairie grasses, willow, and river cane we wove mats we spread across frames made of slender branches to shelter us from the rain and snow. The People were well fed, living on the many crops we grew; berries, roots, and nuts we gathered; and fish and animals we hunted.

But there was something missing.

"We need direction," said the Wa-zha-zhe.

We looked at the world around us. We saw the way the animals and insects lived. These beings each knew their place on the earth and seemed content to occupy it.

"Let us choose a being to guide us," the clans said. "And whichever we choose will be our life symbol. This symbol will be our guiding force, our beauty, our bravery, our courage, our part of the earth."

Most of the clans sent out runners immediately, hoping to take the best life symbols as their own. But one clan was late.

The clan members chose their finest runner to go out and explore. His feats as a seasoned warrior and hunter were proudly tattooed on his hands, wrists, arms, and back. Knowing the importance of his mission, the warrior dabbed his temples, ear-lobes, and lips with paint, and tied his breastplate, a small, reddish-orange disk made of hide, around his chest. Armed with his bow, arrows, and a bag of seeds and herbs, he set out, not knowing his destination, his destiny, or when he would return.

By the time this runner was ready to leave, runners from other clans were returning.

"I saw a deer by the stream," one runner called out. "The deer is swift and sure. The deer will be the life symbol for my clan."

"I saw a buffalo on the prairie," said another runner. "The buffalo is a majestic creature. My clan will take the buffalo as its life symbol."

"I saw an eagle swoop down from high above the clouds and capture a tiny mouse," said another. "This sharp-eyed hunter will be our life symbol."

The runners continued to return, delighted to have claimed all the best symbols for themselves.

"What kind of life symbol is left for us?" asked the late clan. "All that is left is possum, coyote, or smelly skunk. Who wants any of them for a life symbol?"

"Search everywhere," the clan leader told the runner. "There is sure to be an important life symbol left for us to claim."

It so happens that this one particular Wa-zha-zhe runner was so busy searching under every bush and in every treetop that he didn't see a spiderweb stretched across the path and ran headlong into it.

"Aiyiii!" he screamed, trying to pull the sticky web off his face and body. Very

annoyed, the runner looked up at the wood spider in the corner of the web. "You little black thing! Why do you build your house over this trail and cause me to run into it?"

"For what are you searching that you cannot see where you are going?" the spider asked.

"I'm looking for a life symbol for my clan," said the runner. "I'm looking for a being to guide us. So get out of the way, you little black thing!"

"Why don't you take me for your clan symbol?" asked the spider.

The runner put his hand over his mouth so the spider wouldn't see him laughing. And then he asked, "Spider, why do you think you would be a good clan symbol, especially of the great Wa-zha-zhe?"

"Where I am, I build my house," the spider replied. "And where I build my house, all things come to it."

The runner recognized the wisdom of the spider's words. He returned to the village to tell his people the important life symbol he had found.

"The spider!" cried the people. "Other runners came back with grand life symbols for their clans. They chose the majestic buffalo, the swift deer, and the sharp-eyed eagle to be their guiding force. What kind of symbol is the spider for the great Wa-zha-zhe?"

"The buffalo is a majestic beast, but he must wander the prairie in search of food," explained the runner. "The deer is swift and sure, but he must spend his days hiding from the hunter. The eagle is a sharp-eyed hunter, but he must roam the skies in search of prey. Only the spider does not wander in search of food. The spider has few enemies, so he does not spend his days hiding."

The people nodded as they began to understand the runner's choice.

"The spider builds his house in a good place and all things come to him. Our Wa-zha-zhe people will be like the spider," said the runner. "No longer will we walk the earth with no direction. We will make our home in this sheltered valley where the rivers flow and the sun shines down on our people. The Wa-zha-zhe will live here in this good place and all things will come to us."

The Hunter and the Spider

A MUSKOGEE LEGEND

⌃⌃⌃⌃⌃

told by Wilburn Hill, *illustrated by* S. D. Nelson

The Muskogees were called Creek by the British because they lived near creeks. They originally came from Alabama and Georgia. A sedentary people, they farmed, gathered nuts and berries, and hunted small game. Their lodges were made of logs with mud or thatched roofs.

The Muskogees believe that having Ochoclonwa, a spider, in the house means good fortune is coming your way. They do not kill spiders, but let them run off, or carry them outside. The Old Ones say if you let a daddy longlegs crawl on you, he takes away whatever sickness you have because he's a little Indian doctor. Some say if you put a spider in your pocket, somewhere down the line you'll get money. If you want to be healthy, catch a spider and eat the body—it's supposed to make you very healthy for one year.

t is said, once there was a great hunter. Though he was the best hunter in the village, the animals were always just a little bit quicker, just a little bit smarter. Day after day, he returned from hunting with empty hands.

One night, unable to stand the cries of his hungry children, the hunter left his lodge. He wandered through the darkness until tiredness overcame him. He fell asleep on a mound of dirt beneath a big tree.

He awoke early the next morning. It was the kind of morning in which dew clings to blades of grass and drips from the trees. The hunter looked up. Spread across the fork between two branches was a glistening spider's web. The hunter sat for a long while admiring it.

"Little Spider," he said. "You have made such a beautiful design. Why do you go to so much trouble to make your web?"

Then the hunter noticed that a fly had become caught in the spider's web. As he watched, the spider climbed down from a corner of the web and patiently wrapped the struggling insect until finally it was totally bound with the spider's slippery thread.

"Smart Spider, you are something to see," said the hunter. "You don't run all over

⌃⌃

wasting arrows and tiring yourself out to catch your food. You have a plan. If I am going to be a great hunter like you, I need a plan, too."

The hunter returned to the village. In a cone-shaped structure called the hot-house, he drank the "black drink," a tea brewed from Yaupon Holly leaves. Once the "black drink" had cleansed his body and the steam-filled quiet of the hothouse had cleared his mind, the hunter came up with a plan.

Back in the woods, he dug a pit. He covered the deep hole with sticks and fallen leaves so it blended with the woodland floor. Carefully, he laid his last bit of dried meat in the center and returned home.

All day and all night, he thought about the trap he'd set. Time after time, he stopped himself from going to the pit by remembering the example set by the spider.

Not before dawn the next day did the hunter allow himself to return to the woods. He heard noises coming from inside the pit. The sticks and leaves he'd used to camouflage the hole were scattered. Cautiously, he approached the pit and looked down. A buck, many seasons old, large enough to feed the entire village, had fallen into the trap.

Thanks to Ochoclonwa, the spider, Muskogee hunters learned to trap their prey. All things take time.

The Legend of the Loom

A NAVAJO LEGEND

told by Sarah Natani, *illustrated by* Baje Whitethorne

Navajos call themselves Dineh, which means "the People." The Navajo nation is the largest North American Indian tribe. They raise crops, and herd sheep and horses. Traditional Navajos live in circular, mud-covered wooden houses called hogans. The doorway to the hogan always faces east to honor the sun.

According to Navajo legend, "When a baby girl is born to your tribe you shall go and find a spider web which is woven at the mouth of some hole; you must take it and rub it on the baby's hand and arm. Thus, when she grows up she will weave, and her fingers and arms will not tire from the weaving" (from Walk in Beauty *by Anthony Berland and Mary Hunt Kahlenberg).*

A Navajo weaver always sits with her legs folded under to the right side. She weaves a spirit line from an interior background to the edge of each rug to allow her "thinking spirit" to escape when the rug is finished.

 In a time not long after the First Man created the mountains and rivers, and put the light in the sky; not long after the First Woman created the sun and the moon; and not long after the Coyote scattered the stars across the heavens, the Navajo called White Shell Woman lived with her people in the land of golden canyons and red rock bluffs.

Father Sky smiled on White Shell Woman's people. In the spring, Corn People blessed the crops with strong stalks and many tassels. In the summer, streams were filled with fish, wildlife flourished, and bushes were heavy with berries. In the fall, the Navajos harvested corn, squash, beans, and watermelon, thanking Mother Earth for her many gifts.

During the long winter when the Ice God blew his cold breath and covered the canyon with snow, White Shell Woman spent her days making clothes from animal skins. Often she roamed the land in search of feathers, bones, and porcupine quills to decorate them.

One morning as the purple blanket of night was just rising from the top of Navajo Mountain, White Shell Woman awoke. She shook her head and stretched.

Last night, like the three nights before, she had not rested well. Her sleep had been filled with dreams.

On the first night, White Shell Woman had dreamed she was a bluebird making her nest. She flew through the canyon picking up twigs and dried grass and fluff from field flowers.

The second night, she dreamed she was a caterpillar creating a cocoon. She wound threads tightly around her green body until she was completely covered.

The third night, she dreamed she was a beaver building a dam. She hurried through the woods gnawing down trees, hauling them to a still spot in the river and packing them together with mud.

On the fourth night, she dreamed she was a spider spinning a glistening white web between the forked branches of a cottonwood tree.

After each night of dreaming, White Shell Woman had awakened restless and confused, feeling the dreams were telling her something, something she should understand, but didn't.

On the morning after the fourth night, White Shell Woman did her chores as fast as she could. She did not spend time tending the crops in the field. She did not throw bits of food to the turkeys and dogs. Hurriedly, she chopped cedar for the fire. She pounded only enough corn for her breakfast. Patting it into a cake, she placed it on a hot stone near the fire to cook. Not bothering to straighten her hogan, White Shell Woman grabbed up the corn cake and a bit of dried deer meat. The canyon was calling her.

Before the sun's white light peeped over the horizon, White Shell Woman was on her way. That morning the Canyon of Only Rocks looked just as it always had. Dust devils danced on the parched red earth. Lizards darted among the rocks while chipmunks scurried about gathering nuts from the piñon trees.

From the top of Spider Rock, smoke curled into the brightening sky. White Shell Woman followed the trail of smoke. Hand over hand she climbed the tall, spindly peak. Peering into the smokehole, she saw an old woman seated at a loom in the earthen chamber below. The woman's face was creased and crumpled. Her protruding teeth, curved like the claws of a bear, were set wide apart.

"Who are you?" asked White Shell Woman.

"I am Spider Woman, the Navajo spirit," was her reply.

"What are you doing, Spider Woman?" asked White Shell Woman.

"As the bird makes its nest, as the caterpillar creates its cocoon, as the beaver builds its dam and the spider spins its web, I am weaving," answered Spider Woman. She patted the ground next to her. "Come and join me."

"I can't fit into your hole," said White Shell Woman.

"Yes, you can," said Spider Woman. Filling her cheeks with air, she blew to the east and the small hole grew larger. She blew to the west and south; the hole became larger still. When Spider Woman blew to the north, the hole opened wide enough for White Shell Woman to enter.

"Will you teach me to weave?" asked White Shell Woman, sitting beside the old woman.

"I will," Spider Woman replied. "That is why I sent for you."

Spider Woman called to her husband, Spider Man. "Come and build a loom for White Shell Woman," she said.

Out of a key-shaped hole in the cave wall, Spider Man appeared, his arms loaded with pieces of wood and strips of hide. A basket filled with colored balls of cotton hung from his shoulder.

Spider Man began to build the loom. While he worked, he told White Shell Woman the story of the loom.

"The four corners of the loom stand for the directions—north, south, east, and west," said Spider Man, tying the wooden poles together with deer hide. "The top bar is Father Sky and the bottom bar is Mother Earth. The two side poles are rain and moisture. The loom is sacred. It symbolizes water, which gives life."

When the loom was finished, Spider Woman prepared it for weaving. "These warp threads are also rain, and the tension cord holding them to the top of the loom is lightning," explained Spider Woman, stringing strands of cotton across the bars of Father Sky and Mother Earth.

For four days, Spider Woman taught White Shell Woman to weave. The first day, they wove a rug the color of the abalone shell for which White Shell Woman was named. The second day, they wove a turquoise rug, the color of the sky. The

third day, they wove a red rug, symbolizing fire and warmth. The fourth day, they wove a black rug, the color of darkness. And Spider Woman said, "You are done."

With only a quarter moon lighting her way, White Shell Woman walked back through the canyon, carrying her loom. She did not hear the lonely howl of the coyotes. She did not feel the sage and tumbleweed tearing at her skirt. In a dream-like trance, she picked her way through the rocks.

When White Shell Woman arrived home, she set up her loom at the west end of her hogan, as Spider Man had instructed her. Sitting with both legs folded at her right side in the traditional Navajo manner, White Shell Woman prepared the loom for weaving. Slowly, she strung the cotton up and down over the top and bottom bars of the loom, taking great care that each warp thread was an equal distance from the next. Then she began to weave, using scraps from the four rugs she and Spider Woman had made. For many days and nights, the *thump, thump, thump* of the comb pounding the yarn was the only sound to be heard coming from White Shell Woman's hogan.

When the rug was half-finished, White Shell Woman realized she had made a mistake in the pattern. She removed several rows of cotton and started weaving again. Four times White Shell Woman undid the rows and four times she rewove them. But each time, the pattern came out wrong. White Shell Woman became angry. She ripped the rug off the loom, tore it to shreds, and threw it out the door of her hogan.

That night, White Shell Woman did not rest well. Her sleep was filled with dreams of weaving. The unfinished rug wrapped around her, pulling her. The ruined cotton strands choked her.

At dawn the next morning, the wind came early. A sound like the tapping of a comb pounding down the cotton threads on a loom woke White Shell Woman. Only the fading embers of yesterday's fire lit the hogan. Her eyes still fogged from sleep, White Shell Woman peered into the orange darkness. Seated at her loom was the bent figure of Spider Woman wrapped in a brightly patterned blanket. The loom had been restrung and she was weaving the rug White Shell Woman had ripped apart the night before.

"From the moment you begin to weave, your thinking spirit enters the rug," explained Spider Woman. "It lives in the spirit line. Even if you quit weaving, even if you rip and tear the rug as you did last night, the spirit remains and will haunt you until the rug is finished. Never give up." Once again, Spider Woman taught White Shell Woman how to finish the rug.

Ever since that time, the Navajo have passed the art of weaving from generation to generation. Spider Woman's advice to "never give up" is carried out by every Navajo weaver, who completes each rug to the very last thread—never cutting the warp. The Navajo way of weaving is a sacred and honored tradition.

Rainbow Makers

AN ACHOMAWI LEGEND

illustrated by Redwing T. Nez

Achomawi (also spelled Achumawi, and pronounced ah-joo-maw-wee) means "from the river." The Achomawi band is one of eleven autonomous bands that comprise the Pit River Tribe. The Achamawis live in the northeastern corner of California, from the Warner Range to Mount Shasta.

Achomawi mythology has no religious significance. Storytelling is an activity like reading a book or watching a film. Traditionally, stories were told mostly by the old people on cold winter days when everyone huddled together in the earth lodge. Children repeated each line of a story, after the narrator, until they learn it completely.

One winter, so many winters ago that even the oldest Indian can't remember, clouds darkened the world. Rain began to fall. Trickles turned into streams. Streams turned into rivers. And the rivers became raging torrents that washed away trees and filled the animals' burrows.

"Where is the blue sky?" the animals wondered.

"I'll find it," said Eagle, and he flew away. The animals waited. Finally Eagle returned. "I flew as far as I could," he said. "But there is only rain. I flew as high as I could, but there are only clouds. I could not find the blue sky."

The rain kept falling.

The Achomawi Indians who lived along the river were worried, too. It had been raining so hard for so long that the Achomawi men couldn't hunt or catch fish. The Achomawi women couldn't dry hides or cook. And the Achomawi children couldn't gather roots or berries.

"Shaman, we must do something to stop the rain," the Achomawis said to the medicine man.

The Shaman put on his finest blue-jay feathers and picked up his turtle-shell rattle. Chanting loudly, his seed-pod and shell anklets jingling, the Shaman danced his finest stop-the-rain dance.

But the rain continued to fall.

"Coyote's been on earth longer than anyone else," said the Shaman. "He will know what to do."

The Achomawis found Coyote huddled at the back of his cave trying to stay dry.

"I will ask Old Man Above to stop the rain," said Coyote. He shook out his matted fur and threw back his head. "Send back the sun," he howled.

The thunder boomed, the lightning cracked, and the rain continued to fall.

"The storm is so loud, Old Man Above can't hear me," said Coyote. "Take your people and climb to the top of Mount Shasta. I will meet you there."

The Achomawis sloshed up the muddy trail to Mount Shasta. Coyote headed down the path to find Spider Woman.

Spider Woman was mending her rain-soaked web when Coyote found her. "Will you help bring back the sun?" asked Coyote.

"I am too old and tired," said Spider Woman. "But my sixty sons live on the branch below. Maybe they can help."

Spider Woman's two youngest sons jumped at the chance to help Coyote. The threesome headed up the mountain.

On the way, they met the two White-Footed Mouse Boys searching the sodden leaves for nuts.

"We're going to the top of Mount Shasta to bring back the sun," called Coyote. "Will you help us?"

"Yes," said the Mouse Boys. They joined the trio trudging up the trail.

Weasel Man poked his head out of a hollow log. The Mouse Boys shuddered as Weasel Man eyed them hungrily.

"We're going to bring back the sun," said Coyote. "Will you come with us?"

Weasel Man, soaked to the skin and too miserable to chase the Mouse Boys, was ready to do his part.

They hadn't gone far when they came upon Red Fox Woman digging mud out of her burrow. When coyote asked her to join them, she replied, "I'll do anything I can to help stop the rain."

"Me, too," said Rabbit Woman, jumping out of a nearby bush where she had been hiding from the fox.

Coyote, the Spider Brothers, the White-footed Mouse Boys, Weasel Man, Red Fox Woman, and Rabbit Woman plodded up the muddy trail. At the top of the mountain, the Achomawis were waiting.

When the animals caught sight of the warriors' weapons, they shivered. "What is your plan, Coyote?" asked the Achomawis.

"Old Man Above didn't see your stop-the-rain dance. He didn't hear my howls for help," said Coyote. "Someone must climb up to the clouds and whisper in his ear."

"Who?" they asked.

"The Spider Brothers," announced Coyote.

"They are the smallest and weakest of all!" everyone said. "How can they reach the clouds, if we can't?"

"It's because they are the smallest that they can reach the clouds," said Coyote. "We will blow them up."

"But how will we get down?" cried the Spider Brothers.

"After you speak with Old Man Above, you can swing down on your webs," explained Coyote. "Shaman, call forth your best bowmen."

Two warriors stepped forward.

"Aim straight and sure," said Coyote. "You must hit the same spot in the clouds."

Side by side, the arrows flew through the air, piercing a hole through the dark clouds. A glimmer of blue sky shone through.

"Now, blow," commanded Coyote.

The Achomawis puffed, Weasel Man wheezed, Red Fox Woman gasped, the White-footed Mouse Boys huffed, and Rabbit Woman sputtered. But they were barely able to lift the Spider Brothers off the ground.

"The climb was too hard and we are too tired," they complained.

"If we are going to blow the Spider Brothers all the way to the sky, we must work together!" howled Coyote. "Now, blow!"

The animals and the Achomawis filled their cheeks with air. The Spider Brothers jumped as high as they could. *Whooooooooooosh!* The Spider Brothers were blasted up into the sky.

Inches from the arrow hole, the air ran out. The Spider Brothers began to fall.

"Blow again!" howled Coyote.

With the last breaths in their bodies, the animals and Achomawis blew. The Spider Brothers stretched out all of their sixteen legs and caught a corner of the cloud.

Everyone cheered as the Spider Brothers disappeared inside the hole.

"What are you doing here?" roared Old Man Above, a lightning bolt clutched in his mighty fist.

The Spider Brothers cringed. "We have a message for you," they squeaked.

The Old Man Above hurled the lightning bolt toward earth. "What did you say? Speak up!" he thundered.

"Please send back the sun!" the Spider Brothers shouted. The Old Man Above scratched his head and looked around. "How did you get here?" he asked.

The Spider Brothers, all of their legs shaking, climbed up Old Man Above's arm and told him the story.

Beaming as brightly as the morning sun, Old Man Above laughed. "Coyote and Man? Weasel and Mouse? Fox and Rabbit? All working together? How wonderful!"

Old Man Above peeked through the arrow hole. "The clouds have cried enough tears," he said. He pulled the sun from his pouch and placed it in the sky.

"Thank you!" cried the Spider Brothers.

"But I can't have the people shooting holes in my clouds and you spiders crawling up here every time you get wet," said the Old Man Above, shaking his finger.

"Perhaps you could give us a sign to let us know when the rain is over," suggested the Spider Brothers.

"Good idea," said Old Man Above. "I'll use a fox tail."

The Spider Brothers looked around. They didn't see a fox tail anywhere.

"You must imagine one," said Old Man Above.

One Spider Brother remembered Red Fox Woman's bushy tail. Suddenly, a red streak arched across the sky.

The other brother thought of Coyote's fuzzy tail and a yellow streak appeared below the red one.

They imagined green forests, blue waters, and the violet sky of twilight. With each thought a new color was added until an enormous, multicolored fox tail glowed in the sky.

"This is my end-of-the-rain sign," Old Man Above declared. "Tell the people and the animals when they see a rainbow fox tail in the sky, they'll know the sun will follow."

From that time to this, Old Man Above has always hung a rainbow fox tail in the sky as an end-of-the-rain sign. And in honor of the brave Spider Brothers, a tiny rainbow glistens in each spiderweb.

Spider, the Fire Bringer

A CHEROKEE LEGEND

∧·∧·∨·∧·∨·∧·∧

told by Shan Goshorn, *illustrated by* Robert Annesley

The Cherokee Nation once occupied an area of nearly forty thousand square miles, including the southern Appalachian Mountains, the Great Smoky Mountains, and what is today eastern Tennessee, western North Carolina, northern Georgia, and Alabama. In 1838–39, during the Trail of Tears, the Cherokees were forcibly moved to Indian Territory (what is now Oklahoma and eastern Texas).

The Cherokees farmed, gathered grasses and berries, fished, and hunted. Their early dwellings were built of poles, covered inside and out with interwoven twigs or a grass and clay mixture.

The Cherokees are the only American Indian tribe with a written alphabet. It was developed in the early 1800s by the American Indian scholar, Sequoyah. By the 1840s, there were two Cherokee newspapers in print.

"Spider, the Fire Bringer" is the only known Cherokee legend featuring the spider figure. Called Grandmother Spider, Spider Woman, Old Spider, and Water Spider, "In all her forms, she is the goddess who brings the light" (from Grandmothers of the Light, *by Paula Gunn Allen).*

A long, long time ago, back in the beginning of time when everything was first created, all the animals lived together. They got along very well and spoke the same language. The animals didn't eat each other, they only ate plants. They would have been happy except for two things, and both of these happened at night.

For one thing, it was a hundred times colder than it ever is now. Even though the animals wore thick fur coats, they would shiver and shake and pile into a big animal heap to try to keep warm.

For another thing, it was a hundred times darker than it ever is now. The animals would hear sounds deep in the woods and be afraid because they couldn't see in the darkness.

One night the Great Spirit looked down from his place in the sky. He saw his animals cold and afraid. He wanted to make life better for them. He decided to create fire.

The Great Spirit reached up into the sky and grabbed a huge handful of lightning. He was just about to throw it back down to the animal village when he stopped. "I won't make this too easy for the animals," said the Great Spirit. "If they work hard for the fire and finally get it, they will take better care of it."

Instead, he threw the lightning far, far away. The lightning hit a tree. The tree caught on fire and began to burn and burn and burn.

Now, this tree was in the middle of a small island and the island was in the middle of a great water. The animals stood at the edge of the water and saw the tree burning.

"Look!" the animals cried. "There's fire out there! If only we had a way to bring the fire back, it would keep us warm at night and help us see in the darkness."

The animals held a council.

"We need a volunteer who's brave and strong," said Chief of the Animals. "Someone who can swim through the water or fly through the air. Someone who can go to the tree and bring back the fire."

All the animals who could fly and all the animals who could swim raised their wings and their paws. "Chief of the Animals!" they shouted. "I can fly! I can swim!"

After thinking carefully, Chief of the Animals said, "I pick Owl."

"Owl is a good choice," the animals agreed. "Owl is brave and strong. Owl will bring back the fire."

Now, Owl didn't have any idea how to bring back the fire. Owl didn't even know what fire looked like. She flew to the island and circled the tree. "If I can get a good look at the fire," she thought, "I can make a plan."

Owl flew over the top of the tree and looked in. Just as she did, a great gust of wind blew a puff of ashes into her face, blinding her.

Owl flew home the best she could. She rubbed the ashes out of her eyes. But no matter how much she rubbed, Owl was unable to get rid of the big white rings around her eyes. And this is why all the owl grandchildren of the great-grandmother Owl have rings around their eyes.

The animals held another council. This time Chief of the Animals chose Crow. Back in the beginning of time, Crow was the color of the earth. Even then, he was known for being very clever.

"Crow is a good choice," agreed the animals. "Crow will bring back the fire."

Crow had a plan. He flew far, far up into the sky. Then he swooped down into the tree and scooped up a wing full of fire.

Now, Crow did not know much about fire. Crow thought he had the fire, but the fire had Crow. Crow began to burn. He fell out of the tree, slapping at his wings and body. Finally he put the fire out, but not until every single feather was burned a glossy black. To this day, that is why all the crow grandchildren of the great-grandfather Crow are black.

At the next council, Chief of the Animals chose Climbing Snake.

"Climbing Snake is a good choice," agreed the animals. "Climbing Snake will bring back the fire."

Climbing Snake swam through the water and climbed the tree.

Now, Climbing Snake realized you couldn't just pick up fire, you had to choose a stick with fire burning on the end of it. He was deciding which stick to choose when he realized he was getting hot—hotter than he had ever been before. Climbing snake began to squirm and twist to get away from the heat. He lost his balance and fell into the tree.

Luckily, Climbing Snake didn't fall on the fire. He landed in a pile of charcoal. He managed to get out of the tree with his life but his entire body was covered with charcoal that would never come off. And that is why all the grandchildren of great-grandfather Climbing Snake are called Black Snake.

Chief of the Animals called another council. "The night is still cold and dark," he said. "We need another volunteer to bring back the fire."

It was quiet in the council house. Through the silence, a tiny voice rang out. "I'll bring back the fire."

"Who said that?" asked Chief of the Animals.

"I did," said Water Spider, coming forward.

Now, this is not the water spider that looks like a mosquito. This water spider is black with hairy legs. She can walk on top of the water or dive down deep into the water.

"How will you bring back the fire?" the animals asked.

"I have a plan," Water Spider answered.

Everyone watched Water Spider walk across the water to the island. When she reached the shore, Water Spider began to spin and weave. After awhile she had made a perfect little bowl. She set it on her back and crawled through a hole in the bottom of the tree.

The blazing fire singed Water Spider's hair and stung her eyes. She didn't know if she could stand the heat long enough to find what she was looking for. Suddenly she saw it—a red-hot ember.

Water Spider set the ember in the bowl. She ran out of the tree, across the island and across the water.

The animals and birds were waiting for her. They blew on the ember and fed it with leaves and twigs. The ember burst into flames and became a beautiful bonfire—one that kept the animals warm at night; one that helped them see in the darkness.

Today, all the water spider grandchildren of great-grandmother Water Spider carry a bowl on their backs and have a red spot where the ember burned. They are proud of the red spot, for it reminds everyone that Water Spider is the Fire Bringer.

Spider Woman Creates the Burro

A HOPI LEGEND

⌃·⌄·⌃·⌄·⌃·⌄·⌃

illustrated by Michael Lacapa

Hopi means "Peaceful Ones" or "all peaceful." The Hopis are located in north-eastern Arizona, where they have lived longer than any other people. The Hopis built houses of stone plastered with mud on top of three mesas, but many of the fields where they farm corn, squash, melons, beans, and cotton are as far away as ten miles in valleys where water is plentiful.

Called Kokyan Wuhti by the Hopi, Grandmother Spider is "a little old gray lady." Halfway down Third Mesa, beside the path to the fields, is a spring. Anyone passing this way must leave a stick as an offering. For here, under a rock by the water, Grandmother Spider makes her home (from American Indian Mythology, *by Alice Marriott and Carol K. Rachlin).*

 Back in the before time, when the earth was new, the Hopi people came up from the First World to search for the Land of the Rising Sun.

Traveling in family groups called clans, they journeyed over mountains, across deserts, and through canyons. The mighty Bear Clan led the way, while the people of the Spider Clan traveled the slowest of all.

Long after the sun had shriveled the last of the desert flowers, the Spider Clan trudged wearily on, hoping to catch up with the rest of the tribe.

Suddenly, a fierce wind began to blow. It whipped the sage and pelted the people with sand. Searching for shelter, the chief spotted a cave. A giant web stretched across its mouth. A spider in the center of the web beckoned to him.

"I am Spider Woman," she said. "Your clan is named for my people. Come into my cave where you will be safe."

Inside, the cave was dark and cool. Water from a hidden spring trickled down the rock walls.

"We are hunting for the Land of the Rising Sun," said the chief. "We are far behind the rest of our tribe because we have so many children and so much to carry."

"I can ease your load," said Spider Woman. "But you must give me something of yourself."

"Whatever I have is yours," the chief answered.

Spider Woman pointed to a room in the back of the cave. "Go into my secret place," she said. "There you will find a water jug. Wash yourself well. Save the dust and skin that rolls off and bring it to me."

After traveling so long, the chief was caked with dirt. He brought Spider Woman a dust-and-skin ball the size of his fist.

Spider Woman spread a sheepskin on the ground and wrapped the ball in it. She nestled the ball in her lap and began chanting a ceremonial creation song. She chanted the song four times. After the fourth time, she covered the ball with her magic web.

Again, Spider Woman began to sing. When she had sung the song four more times, the fleecy white ball trembled. It rolled this way and that. As the Spider Clan watched, a tiny gray animal with four tiny legs popped out of the ball.

"This animal is a burro," said Spider Woman. "It will carry your heavy loads."

"The burro is small and weak like us," said the chief. "How can it help?"

"Wait and you will see," said Spider Woman. She carried the tiny burro into her secret place.

For four days, Spider Woman cared for the burro. She fed it special food and rubbed it with a magic ointment to make it grow. At the end of that time, she gave the full-grown burro to the Spider Clan. Packing their belongings upon the burro's back, the clan continued their journey to the Land of the Rising Sun.

Since that time, the burro has lived among the Hopi people, easing their load.

How the Half-Boys Came to Be

A KIOWA LEGEND

⌃·⌃·⌃·⌃·⌃·⌃

illustrated by Robert Annesley

The Kiowas are traditionally a nomadic tribe, following the bison north to Montana in the summer and as far south as northern Mexico in winter.

"How the Half-Boys Came to Be," sometimes called "How the Split-Boys Came To Be," is part of the Kiowa sacred cycle. Some Kiowa believe it's sacrilegious for the sacred cycle stories to be published, printed, or talked about by non-Kiowa. The sections appearing here, "How the Half-Boys Came to Be" and "The Great Flood," have been previously published, and permission has been granted for their use by Evans Ray Satepauhoodle.

In the Kiowa language, the word p'ee (pronounced pie) connotes fire and heat; it's also the word for porcupine. In this Southern Kiowa version, the Sun is interpreted to be a porcupine. In other versions, the Sun takes on the form of a yellow or red bird.

Spider Woman, also called Grandmother Spider, is often depicted as a little old gray lady (although she can change shapes to become anything she wants to be). She is a helpmate and teacher to the Kiowa.

The Half-Boys are of supernatural parentage on one side. They are "perceived to be the duality basic to all men and all religions" (from American Indian Mythology, by Alice Marriott and Carol K. Rachlin).

This happened a long time ago, when the Kiowa people lived on the eastern edge of the Rocky Mountains in the area known today as Wyoming.

A man and his wife had one child, a baby girl. They took very good care of her.

One day the couple had to take a trip that was a day's ride away. They thought the trip would be too long for the little girl, so they asked a friend to watch her.

"Sure, sure, I'll watch her," said the friend.

"Please take very good care of my baby girl," said the mother.

"She'll be fine," said the friend. "Now, go on."

For awhile the friend was content to play with the little girl. But soon she tired of looking after her. "If I put her in the cradleboard and hang it in a tree," she thought, "the wind will rock her to sleep."

And that's just what she did.

Strapped in her cradleboard, swaying in the breeze, the little girl was watching the clouds go by when she saw a porcupine. The round, prickly porcupine smiled at the little girl. She giggled at the funny-looking creature. The porcupine stood on its head and did somersaults and cartwheels.

The little girl liked the porcupine so much she wiggled out of her cradleboard and climbed over to him. The porcupine started crawling higher into the tree. The little girl crawled after him. The porcupine climbed all the way up to the top of the tree. When the porcupine and the little girl reached the top, the tree started growing. The tree grew so tall, it touched the sky. When it touched the sky, the porcupine jumped up and turned himself into a man.

This man was the Sun and he had magical powers. He turned the little baby girl into a woman and took her to be his wife.

"I have a job to do," the Sun explained to his wife. "Every morning I travel to the west and every night I come home to rest. During the day while I'm away, do whatever you wish. I have only one rule: Never go near the bush that has been cropped off by a buffalo."

After a time, the Sun and his wife had a baby boy. The woman was happy because now she wouldn't have to be alone all day. She tied the baby to her back and explored the strange sky world.

One day, the woman was digging for potatoes and came upon the bush that had been cropped off by a buffalo. "My husband told me never ever to go near this bush," she said. "I wonder why?"

Some of the bush's roots were showing. The woman couldn't help herself. She dug around the roots. She saw a glimmer of light. She peered down through the roots and could see the world she had come from.

Excitedly, the woman dug up the bush and put it to the side. Through the hole in the sky, she watched her people playing games and singing songs.

The woman had lonesome feelings and remembered. She put the bush back and picked up her baby. "I wonder how I can get down there to see my people," she said.

The woman began to braid a rope of sinew. Each night when her husband came home, she hid the rope in a basket. Every day while the Sun was away, she braided the rope longer and longer. Finally, the rope was long enough to reach from the sky down to the earth.

The next morning, after the Sun went to work, the woman took her baby and the bundle of rope to the bush. She wrapped the rope around herself and her baby several times. Then she took the other end and wrapped it securely around a tree.

The woman lowered herself through the hole. But she had wrapped the rope around herself and around her baby and around the tree so many times that she didn't have enough rope to reach the earth. She was stuck between the sky and the earth. She couldn't go up and she couldn't go down. She hung there all day, swinging back and forth, back and forth.

When the Sun came home, his tipi was empty, the fire was cold, and there was no sign of a meal. He searched for his wife and baby, but they were nowhere to be found.

"I wonder if she's gone over to the bush that's been cropped off by the buffalo," he thought.

When the Sun looked down into the hole and saw his wife and baby swinging back and forth, back and forth, he knew he'd been deceived.

The Sun was very angry. He thought he'd done the woman a favor by bringing her up into the sky to live with him. He picked up a medicine wheel and threw it down at the woman. The wooden hoop rolled down the rope, bounced over the baby, and struck the woman on her forehead. She fell to the ground and died.

The baby survived the fall because he was magical—part Sun and part human.

Frightened and alone in this strange world, the little boy stayed with his mother until he became so hungry he crawled away to find food. Not far from where he had fallen to earth, the boy came upon an empty lodge. The lodge was the home of Grandmother Spider. She had left some food out to dry. The boy gobbled up the food and crawled back to his mother.

That evening, when Grandmother Spider returned, she saw the food was gone and there were little handprints and footprints all over the place. "What is this?" she

asked. "I don't have any children. I wonder who this child is. Is it a girl or a boy?"

The next morning, before Grandmother Spider went hunting, she set some food out for the baby in case it returned. She also set out a ball for a girl baby and a bow and arrow for a boy baby.

Sure enough, the baby returned looking for something to eat. He saw the ball and passed it by. But when he saw the bow and arrow, he couldn't resist. He picked them up and ran back to his mother.

When Grandmother Spider saw that the bow and arrow were gone, she said, "Oh, now I know this child is a boy baby. It will be a hard job to raise him, but I would like to have a boy."

Instead of going hunting the next day, Grandmother Spider hid, and when the baby boy came to her lodge, she captured him. The boy cried and screamed and bit her because he didn't want her; he wanted his mother.

Grandmother Spider began to sing. Her singing calmed the boy. "Call me Grandmother," she told him, "for I am the Spider Woman, the mother and comforter of all living things. And I will call you *Tah'-lee*, which means little boy."

In time, Grandmother Spider and Tah'-lee became familiar with one another and she raised him. She taught him everything he needed to know to be a good, strong, brave young man.

One day, when Tah'-lee was about twelve or thirteen years old, Grandmother Spider gave him the medicine wheel that had killed his mother. She taught him to roll the wooden hoop on the ground and throw a spear through the hole in the center to practice his aim.

"Never throw this hoop in the air," she warned him, "especially when it's windy. Always roll the hoop along the ground."

But as children will, as soon as Grandmother Spider turned her back, Tah'-lee threw that medicine wheel high into the sky. It went up so high it disappeared. Tah'-lee waited and waited.

Finally, the medicine wheel came back—it came back so hard and so fast that Tah'-lee never saw it. It hit Tah'-lee in the middle of the forehead and split him in two.

But the medicine wheel didn't hurt Tah'-lee because he was magical—he was part Sun and part human. Tah'-lee was split lengthwise into two boys. They were not twins, but half-boys with magical powers—one of the sky, the other of the earth.

When Grandmother Spider saw she had two boys instead of one, she cried, "Oh, no! It was hard enough taking care of one boy. Now I have two boys to take care of!"

Wihio Meets One of the Little People

A CHEYENNE LEGEND

∧·∧·∨·∧·∨·∧·∧

illustrated by Benjamin Harjo

The earliest-known home of the Cheyennes, an Algonquian tribe of the high plains, was present-day Minnesota, between the Mississippi and Minnesota Rivers. They started out living in villages, farming, and making pottery. Around the seventeenth century, like most other Plains tribes, the Cheyennes adopted a nomadic lifestyle.

"Wihio Meets One of the Little People" is both a white man's story and a spider story. Though many believe wihio means "spider," it actually means "sod dweller" or "earth lodge dweller," which is what the Cheyennes called white men. The word for spider is not wihio, but vihio. The "soddies" settlers built reminded the Cheyenne of the burrows of spiders that live underground. The two words, wihio and vihio, have come to mean the same thing.

The Little People were a group of medicine men who, because they were so small, did not have to do ordinary work. They were left to spend all their days and nights praying, fasting, and sitting in the sweat lodge. Over time, their medicine became so powerful that they became afraid someone would capture it, and use it wrongly. So the Little People moved into the mountains that we now call the Rockies, and made their homes in caves so high up they could see all of Cheyenne country.

Cheyenne stories are told around the campfire. When one man runs out of stories, or tires, he asks, "Can anyone tie another to it?" In this manner, the storytelling continues. When the stories are finished, they end with "This cuts it off."

**W**ihio was traveling down by the creek in search of some mischief. He came upon a man looking at a tree. Though the man was dressed in Cheyenne clothing and looked like a Cheyenne, he was very small.

He must be one of the Little People, thought Wihio, one of the medicine men who lives in the caves high up in the mountains. I wonder if they are as powerful as people say.

The little man walked over to the tallest, straightest tree. After carefully examining it, the man kicked the tree and knocked it over. He kicked it once and the tree fell!

The little man began forming an enormous arrow out of the trunk.

"Little Brother, what are you doing with that tree?" asked Wihio.

"Use your eyes and you can see," said the little man, shaping the end of the tree, which was as large around as Wihio himself, into a sharp point.

"You can't expect me to believe a little brother like you can shoot an arrow as thick and long as this," said Wihio.

Ignoring Wihio, the little man continued working, chopping the limbs off the trunk.

"If you can throw such an arrow so many times bigger than yourself, show me," said Wihio. "Shoot at me."

"I might kill you," said the little man.

Wihio laughed. "I knew it. You're too small to lift an arrow so big." And Wihio turned to walk away.

"I will shoot at you," called the little man. He pointed to a mountain in the far distance. "Walk toward that hill."

Wihio walked a little way and stopped. "Is this far enough?" he asked.

"No," said the little man. "You are too close. You might get hurt."

Wihio laughed, but he followed the little man's directions and continued walking. Four times Wihio stopped, and four times the little man instructed him to go farther.

Finally, Wihio reached the top of the mountain. "This is far enough," he shouted. "If I go any farther, I cannot hear your voice. Throw the arrow."

When Wihio saw how easily the little man lifted the arrow, he became alarmed. And when the little man brought the arrow back to throw, Wihio cried out, "Little Brother, I knew you could pick up the arrow. I was only playing with you. You don't have to shoot at me now."

"Oh, you tricky Wihio, you have out-tricked yourself," said the little man. "It is too late. Once I have taken aim, I must shoot the arrow or I will lose my medicine." The arrow flew from the little man's hands with such force it made the trees in the forest bend.

As the arrow came toward him, Wihio started to scream and run away. No matter which way Wihio ran, the arrow followed him. Nearer and nearer the arrow flew, pointing straight at Wihio. With the arrow almost upon him, Wihio threw himself to the ground.

The arrow arched down and struck Wihio, pushing his body deep into the earth until only his head stuck out.

The little man walked up to Wihio. "You should not have doubted my medicine," he said.

"Little Brother, you are a good shot," said Wihio. "Please help me out of this hole and I will never try to trick you again."

The little man pulled Wihio out of the earth and sent him on his way.

Iktomi and Buzzard

A LAKOTA LEGEND

told by Edward Ramon, *illustrated by* Redwing T. Nez

The Lakotas are part of the Sioux family, originally inhabiting what is now the southern half of Minnesota. They were woodland and prairie people living in bark lodges who farmed, fished, and hunted. After the introduction of the horse, the Lakotas became a nomadic people. They lived in tipis and abandoned farming in favor of bison hunting.

Iktomi, the Sioux trickster figure, is both spider and man. As a spider, he is greedy and calculating. As a man, he is handsome and beautiful and always wants to do good things. He weaves sinister webs and is often caught in his own traps. Iktomi's best gifts are the lessons he teaches through his mistakes.

Iktomi was sitting under a tree, smoking his pipe. It was a beautiful day, and Iktomi loved beautiful things.

Iktomi looked up at the sky. His friend Buzzard was flying high above Mother Earth. "I wish I could fly," he said. "I know, I will think hard and my brother Buzzard will come down and take me for a ride."

Iktomi began to think, and he thought and he thought, "Come down, Buzzard, come down."

Sure enough, Buzzard began to make a big circle. He circled lower and lower and lower and landed on the earth beside Iktomi.

"Iktomi, get on my back and I will take you for a ride," Buzzard said.

Iktomi climbed onto Buzzard's back. Buzzard flapped his wings and flew again to great heights above Mother Earth. While Buzzard circled slowly, Iktomi looked down. He saw that everything was beautiful within the great hoop. "The world is beautiful, just like me," said Iktomi. "I am very beautiful and I should be surrounded by beautiful things."

Iktomi looked straight ahead and gasped. "Oh, what is that ugly thing? It's red and lumpy. It looks as though it's been scalded by the sun. There are no feathers, only coarse hairs. Oh, it is the head of Buzzard! It is so ugly!"

Though the Lakota people have no swear words, they, like any other culture or people, make obscene gestures. So, in a great gesture of mockery and ridicule, Iktomi clenched his fist, laid down his thumb, and rapidly pushed open his hand, making a "throws away" gesture. And then he did it again—he clenched his fist, laid down his thumb, and rapidly pushed open his hand. This was an even more obscene gesture because it was done behind Buzzard's back. Iktomi laughed while he made fun of his friend.

Now, to help Buzzard search for food, the Creator had given him a wonderful gift—he could see to great distances. So while he was flying about, Buzzard looked down upon the earth far below and saw the shadow of Iktomi's hands making that gesture.

"Iktomi mocks me," Buzzard thought. "Surely, I can find a gift to give him."

A great distance away, Buzzard saw a charred tree trunk where one of the Standing People had been torn apart by wind and lightning—a lone tree in the middle of the prairie.

Buzzard dove toward the Mother Earth. Just as he flew above the stump, he flipped over. Iktomi fell from Buzzard's back and landed upside down in the splinters of the stump.

Iktomi struggled and struggled, but he was trapped, wedged in the wood. "Help! Help!" he cried out. "I cannot get free!"

Wakiyan botan, lightning gives birth to sound. It began to rain. Big raindrops fell upon the stump. The wood began to swell, squeezing Iktomi tighter and tighter and tighter.

Iktomi was pitiful in his crying. "Oh, this is a horrible punishment. I should not have made fun of Buzzard. My friend was giving me a ride and I mocked him."

Iktomi became more and more ashamed. He grew smaller and smaller. He began to pray for forgiveness. As Iktomi became more humble, he grew even more small. Finally he was small enough to crawl out of the stump.

"Because I have become humble, I have become small," said Iktomi. "I have freed myself from my trouble."

Wash-ste-lo, goodness has helped me.

Dreamcatcher Story

A MUSKOGEE LEGEND

told by Wilburn Hill, *illustrated by* Benjamin Harjo

Stories about dreamcatchers are shared by almost every Native American tribe, from Alaska to South America. Each tribe has a slightly different version of the dreamcatcher story, and each makes dreamcatchers somewhat differently. All dreamcatchers, however, are made of some type of cording woven onto a hoop. Some are decorated with beads and feathers. The Muskogee make their dreamcatchers with a hole in the center, believing the web will catch the good thoughts and dreams, while the bad ones fall through the hole.

ong ago, in a Muskogee village, there lived a crippled boy. One of his legs was much shorter than the other. He could not walk or play like the other children. His mother and father loved him very much and took special care of him.

One sunny afternoon, his mother carried the boy to the bank surrounding a sunken playing field, where he sat alone on a blanket and watched the children playing. Using sticks with rawhide bowls woven onto one end, tall, wiry boys ran up and down the field whacking a deerskin ball.

"I wish I could play stickball, too," said the boy.

Just then cheers of victory resounded as the ball hit the center pole. Enviously, the boy watched the winning teammates congratulate each other.

"I wish I had friends to laugh with," he said.

He was sitting there feeling sorry for himself when his *posah*, his grandmother, came by. "What's the matter, baby?" she asked.

"I wish I could play like other kids," the boy said.

That night, after the food had been eaten and all the dishes had been put away, Posah sat the boy in her lap. "Sometimes, if you really believe in a dream, it comes true," she said. "I'm going to make something special to help you catch your dream."

Posah gathered four thin sticks and some sinew. She soaked them in water. When they were flexible, she tied the sticks end to end and bent them into a circle. Then she began to weave the sinew across the wooden circle, leaving a small hole in the center.

"It looks like a spiderweb," said the boy.

"It is called a dreamcatcher," said Posah. "Our people learned to make it from watching *Posah Ochoclonwa*, Grandmother Spider. I am your grandmother and I am making this one for you. When you sleep, the dreamcatcher will catch all your good dreams, good thoughts, in its spider web."

"You left a hole in the middle," said the boy.

"Through that hole, all your bad dreams, bad thoughts, can escape," she said.

Posah carried the boy into the lodge house. She placed the dreamcatcher on a post above his sleeping space. "While you sleep, your dream of being like other children can be caught in the dreamcatcher. But remember, you really have to believe. There can't be room for doubt, not one little drop of doubt."

Night after night, the boy tried to believe. But, as they do, doubts crept into his mind about whether the dreamcatcher would work. Each morning, when he woke, one leg was still shorter than the other.

The boy complained to his posah. "The dreamcatcher does not work."

"The dreamcatcher will only work if your belief is strong," Posah answered. "You must believe with all your heart."

That night when he was in bed, the boy asked the Creator to make him whole. And that night, in his dream, the boy was just like the other children; his legs were strong. In his dream, he ran, laughed, and played stickball. The dream seemed so real. "I know I'm just dreaming," he thought, "but it's a good dream."

The boy woke early in the morning. While he waited for his mother to come and pick him up, he remembered his dream. "I wish it had been real," he said.

As he had done every morning since Posah had made the dreamcatcher, the boy pulled back his sleeping blanket and looked at his legs. It seemed to him that his short leg had grown.

"Am I still dreaming?" he wondered. "Or did my dream come true?" He looked up at the dreamcatcher. "I want to try."

The boy stood up. He stood up all by himself and he walked.

Ever since then, grandmothers have made dreamcatchers for their babies so that good fortune will come their way.

Story Sources

Versions of "The Great Flood" and "How the Half-Boys Came to Be" appeared in *Kiowa Voices, Vol. II: Myths, Legends, and Folktales*, by Maurice Boyd (Texas Christian University Press, 1983). Also, both stories were told to us by various storytellers of the Southern Kiowa Nation. Permission to publish them was secured by Evans Ray Satepauhoodle, a tribal elder and member of the Black Legging Society, and he also authenticated the stories. Mr. Satepauhoodle is head of the Kiowa Language Program in Carnegie, Oklahoma, and Tulsa. He is also author of a Kiowa language guide.

"How the Tewas Found Their True Home" was published in *American Indian Mythology*, by Alice Mariott and Carol K. Rachlin (Thomas Y. Crowell Co., 1968). This version was verified by Michael Lacapa. Mr. Lacapa, of Apache, Hopi, and Tewa descent, is an award-winning author and illustrator of children's books.

"Swift Runner and Trickster Tarantula" appeared in *Tepee Tales of the American Indian*, by Dee Brown (Holt, Rinehart, and Winston, 1979). Our version was verified by Zuni Rita Edaakie.

A version of "How the Spider Got Its Web" appeared in *How the People Sang the Mountains Up: How and Why Stories*, by Maria Leach (New York: Viking Press, 1967). Our version was presented at the November 28, 1995, Council meeting of the Bear River Band of the Rohnerville Rancheria, at which time it was approved and permission for its publication was granted.

"Osage Spider Story" appears here as told by Sky Clan Osage Archie Mason, Jr. In addition to being a storyteller, Mr. Mason is director of Indian education in Tulsa, Oklahoma, and the advisor to Native American students at Tulsa University.

"The Hunter and the Spider" and "Dreamcatcher Story" were told by Wilburn Hill, Wind Clan Muskogee. Mr. Hill is the Artistic Director of Mahenwahdose Productions, Inc., True Native American Theater. A traditional storyteller, Mr. Hill was chosen as a small boy by his clan to follow in the footsteps of his father, uncle, and grandfather. Mr. Hill also serves on the board of directors of the American Indian Theater Company and is committed to continuing Muskogee oral traditions by working with Native American children.

"The Legend of the Loom" was told by Navajo Sarah Natani. Ms. Natani raises her own sheep, shears them, and dyes the wool herself. Ms. Natani teaches adult education in Shiprock, New Mexico. A master weaver, Sarah learned to weave from her mother, whose great-grandmother taught her to weave.

Kelly Bennett heard "Rainbow Makers" for the first time while fishing at Dad's Camp on the mouth of the Klamath River in the early 1970s. Radley Davis, a member of the Illmawi Band of the Pit River Tribe, shared this version of "Rainbow Makers" with tribal members, and permission to use it here was granted. Other versions of this legend appeared in *Someone Saw a Spider,* by Shirley Climo (Thomas Y. Crowell, 1985) and in *Stories California Indians Told* by Anne Fisher (Parnassus Press, 1957).

"Spider, the Fire Bringer" was told by Shan Goshorn. A Wolf Clan Cherokee from North Carolina, Ms. Goshorn is a storyteller and award-winning artist. A member of the State Arts Council of Oklahoma Artist-in-Residence Program, Ms. Goshorn travels nationally and internationally, speaking on the political and social issues of American Indians.

"Spider Woman Creates the Burro" was told by Hopi Alph Secakuku, who points out that this enduring legend is unusual in that it explains the appearance of an animal brought to the Hopi mesas by the outsiders, namely, the Spaniards. Many Hopis consider the burro a symbol of the difficulties they encountered with the Spaniards. Mr. Secakuku is an artist and lecturer on the subject of Hopi tradition and culture. This legend also appeared in *Voices of the Winds,* by Margot Edmonds and Ella E. Clark (*Facts on File,* 1989).

A version of "Wihio Meets One of the Little People" appeared in *By Cheyenne Campfires,* by George Bird Grinnell (University of Nebraska Press, 1971). This version was approved by Sam Hart, a storyteller and member of the Cheyenne-Arapaho tribes of Oklahoma.

"Iktomi and Buzzard" was told by Edward Ramon. He is a Lakota-Comanche and lives in Chelsea, Oklahoma. Mr. Ramon is a storyteller, psychologist, craftsman, playwright, songwriter, poet, and author of a book entitled *Scars and Stripes Forever.* A Vietnam veteran, Mr. Ramon was honored by the 101st Congress as a Native American war hero (one of three most highly decorated).

Editor

✦◦✦◦✦◦✦◦✦

JILL MAX is the pseudonym for the writing team of Kelly Bennett and Ronnie Davidson. They live in Tulsa, Oklahoma, where they have done extensive research on Native American customs and lore at the Gilcrease Museum. The co-authors of five books and numerous articles, they have traveled extensively, collecting Native American crafts and studying various cultures. *Spider Spins a Story* is the result of their interest in exploring the recurrence of the spider as a unifying thread in the literature of diverse Native American cultures.

Illustrators

✦◦✦◦✦◦✦◦✦

ROBERT ANNESLEY is of Cherokee descent. He is a lifetime member of the American Indian and Cowboy Artists of America. The recipient of over 170 national awards, Annesley has art on display at the National Cowboy Hall of Fame and the Royal Academy of Fine Arts in London.

BENJAMIN HARJO is of Seminole and Cherokee descent. His award-winning art has been featured in *Southwest Art* and *Persimmon Hill*, the official publication of the National Cowboy Hall of Fame, and he has consistently garnered top honors for his work at the Indian Market in Santa Fe, New Mexico.

MICHAEL LACAPA is of Apache, Hopi, and Tewa descent. He is an award-winning author-illustrator. He illustrated *The Mouse Couple, The Flute Player,* and with his wife, Kathleen, as co-author, he wrote and illustrated *Less Than Half, More Than Whole,* all from Northland Publishing. He received the 1991 Arizona Author Award from the Arizona State Library Association.

S. D. NELSON is of Standing Rock Sioux descent. His award-winning illustrations have appeared on several book and compact disc covers. His wildlife art has been recognized with awards from several organizations including the Rocky Mountain Elk Foundation and Ducks Unlimited. He has traveled to South America to study the pre-Columbian rock art of the region, where he was struck by the similarities between the rock art of the Andean highlands and that of the Southwest.

REDWING T. NEZ is of Navajo descent. As the author-illustrator of *Forbidden Talent*, from Northland Publishing, Nez was named a Storyteller Award finalist by Western Writers of America. His work and words appear in *Enduring Traditions: Art of the Navajo*, also from Northland Publishing.

BAJE WHITETHORNE is of Navajo descent. He is the award-winning author-illustrator of *Sunpainters: Eclipse of the Navajo Sun*, and the illustrator of *Monster Birds: A Navajo Folktale* and *Monster Slayer: A Navajo Folktale*, all from Northland Publishing. He received the 1996 Arizona Author Award from the Arizona State Library Association.